Chapter One

Sir Garibald lived with his dragon Hot Nose in a dark, creepy castle in the mountains.

The castle was especially dark and creepy at night. Then it was lit only by candles and Hot Nose's fiery breath. Sir Garibald and Hot Nose kept nearly jumping out of their skins with fright.

Even so, they never thought of changing things. Until …

One day Sir Garibald was asked to visit the nearest school and tell the children about knights in the olden days.

He told them about castles, and rescuing people, and fighting dragons.

Afterwards the children showed him one of their school video games. It was about a knight.

Sir Garibald loved the video game. The children

MARJORIE NEWMAN

Sir Garibald

MACDONALD YOUNG BOOKS

showed him some more. Sir Garibald
was still playing the games at home time.

It was quite late before he hurried back
up the mountain to his dark, creepy castle.

"Hot Nose!" he yelled, stumbling over
the front doorstep because he couldn't
see it properly (*and* because he had very
big feet). "Hot Nose! Where are you?
We've got to get some video games!"

Hot Nose had hidden under the
kitchen table when he heard all the
shouting. Now he came out. He lit ten
candles at once with his fiery breath.

"Video games?" he asked. "Played on computers?"

"Yes! Yes!" cried Sir Garibald.

"Then we'll need electricity," said Hot Nose. "This castle hasn't *got* electricity."

"Oh," said Sir Garibald. With a sinking feeling he realized Hot Nose was right. "Never mind!" he cried. "We shall have electricity! I'll get it put in!"

"Electric lights, and hot water, and all that sort of thing?" asked Hot Nose.

"All that sort of thing!" promised Sir Garibald.

"And the castle won't be creepy any more?" asked Hot Nose.

"Not a bit creepy," promised Sir Garibald.

"Hooray!" shouted Hot Nose. "How much will it cost?"

"Ah," said Sir Garibald. "Quite a lot, I expect. Fetch your savings, Hot Nose!"

Quietly, Hot Nose fetched his savings from his secret hiding place.

Noisily, bumping about in the darkness – and tripping over his big feet quite a lot – Sir Garibald fetched *his* savings from his secret hiding place.

They tipped the money onto the kitchen table, and looked at it in the candlelight.

It was a very small pile.

"I'm afraid that won't be enough," sighed Sir Garibald.

"I'm sure it won't be enough," agreed Hot Nose. "We'll have to get more."

"How?" asked Sir Garibald.

Hot Nose thought for a moment. Then he smiled a crafty smile.

"In the olden days," he remarked, "knights had the very bad habit of fighting dragons."

"Yes," agreed Sir Garibald, puzzled.

"And got a *reward*," said Hot Nose.

"Yes," agreed Sir Garibald.

"Well ..." said Hot Nose. He whispered in Sir Garibald's ear.

Sir Garibald began to smile.

"But . . is that quite . . honest?" he asked. "And will it work?"

Chapter Two

Early next morning Hot Nose flapped quietly away from the castle. It was very cold, but he was too full of his plan to notice. He flew on until presently, down below, he saw the village of Nettleford. It was what he had been looking for. No one in Nettleford would know himself and Sir Garibald.

He zoomed down onto the church roof.

The wind blew cold. Now and again a car drove along the narrow winding street to the village square. Aunty Flo stood in the phone box, talking to a friend who lived in the nearby village of Greenways. Everything was peaceful.

Hot Nose grinned. Then, suddenly, he stood up, flapped his wings, and took off. Round and round the village he flew, just above the roof tops. Every now and again he let out a mighty 'Whoooosh!' of fire.

Down below there was uproar. Drivers looked up, and their cars crashed into hedges or ditches. Babies cried. Cats meowed. Dogs yelped. Ducks quacked. Aunty Flo screamed.

The children in the village school rushed to look out of the windows.

"It's a dragon!" they cried.

Hot Nose had a marvellous time, soaring and whooshing and flapping his wings.

The policeman

came running out. He radioed for the
fire brigade. Then he called to Hot Nose
on his loudspeaker to come down.

The firefighters arrived. They aimed
their hoses at Hot Nose. But they
couldn't aim them as fast as Hot Nose
could twist and turn. The firefighters got
in a terrible mess.

The children laughed
so much they could
hardly stand up.

He landed in the castle courtyard.

Sir Garibald rushed out, tripping over his big feet.

"What happened?" he cried.

"It all went splendidly!" said Hot Nose. "We're ready for Part Two!"

While Hot Nose got himself a quick (but large) snack, Sir Garibald got out his old motor-bike.

It was hard to ride a motor-bike wearing a suit of armour and carrying a sword. Sir Garibald fell off once or twice. Then he got his balance, and spluttered away towards Nettleford.

Presently Hot Nose took off again, flying after Sir Garibald.

"Really?" said Sir Garibald. He looked
up. Hot Nose let out another "whoosh"
of fire.

"Aaaaaah!" screamed the
villagers.

"Stop that, dragon!" ordered Sir
Garibald.

Hot Nose let out another 'whoosh!',
and flew down to sit across the roof of
a car.

"Aaaaaah!" screamed the villagers again.

"Oooooooh!" cried the children,
nearly tumbling out of the windows in
excitement.

The mayor stepped forward.

"Something must be done," he said. "At
once. Sir. I can see you are a knight. I know
that knights fight dragons. They are better
at fighting dragons than even the police or
the fire brigade. If you will get rid of this
dragon we will give you a big reward."

Sir Garibald gulped.

"Is it a f . . f . . fierce, wild dragon?" he trembled.

Chapter Four

"It looks like a *very* fierce, wild dragon!" said the people. "Please help us, before it eats us or sets fire to our houses!"

Sir Garibald tried to think. He didn't want to tell the villagers of Nettleford he'd been tricking them.

He *did* want to help the people from Greenways.

He looked around. "Hot Nose?"

Hot Nose was hiding amongst the bushes. His voice was muffled. "I can see him. He's in Greenways' market place," he said. "You can easily fight him. I'll wait here!"

Sir Garibald had to make up his mind.

Chapter Five

Slowly Sir Garibald rode back to the
village. Slowly he got off his motor-bike.
Slowly he handed the reward money
back to the mayor.

Hot Nose was watching. He couldn't
bear it! Giving the money back?

The Mayor and all the villagers were
puzzled.

"Just along there!" they said. And they hid.

Trembling, Sir Garibald got off his motor-bike and crept into the market place. Hot Nose could hardly bear to watch.

The second dragon was stamping its feet and breathing out fire.

In a high, trembling voice Sir Garibald called, "D . . D . . D . . Dragon! G . . Go away! Or I'll f . . f . .f . . fight you!"

The dragon stood still and looked at him.

"Fight me! What for?"

"For f . . f . . frightening people," said Sir Garibald. "S . . s . . stamping

your feet, and b . . b . . breathing out fire."

"How misunderstood can a dragon be?" glared the dragon. "Never judge a person till you know them! I'm not trying to frighten people. I'm cold. I'm trying to keep warm!"

Sir Garibald looked doubtfully at the dragon. Was it telling the truth?

"In any case, I never eat people," added the dragon. "I'm a vegetarian. But I do feel the cold."

It blew out more fire, trying to warm its feet. Sir Garibald was sorry for it. He thought hard. Then he said, "Wait!"

He unwound the long woolly scarf he always wore when he rode his motor-bike. Quickly he wound it round the dragon's neck.

Then he sat down and took off his shoes. He pulled off the warm stretchy

socks he always wore when he rode his
motor-bike. He fitted his socks onto the
dragon's back feet.

Next he reached into his pockets and
pulled out the warm stretchy gloves he
always had with him when he rode his
motor-bike. He tugged them onto the
dragon's front feet.

"How's that?" he asked.
"Much better!" smiled the dragon.

"Thank you. I can fly on now. I'm a long way from home, you know."

Sir Garibald stepped back. The dragon flapped its wings, rose into the air and flew off.

The villagers saw it go. They came running up.

"Well done!" they cried.

Hot Nose zoomed down.

"Aaaaah!" screamed the villagers.

Then they remembered it was only Hot
Nose.

Hot Nose was thinking about
rewards...

The mayor of Nettleford stepped
forward.

"Sir Knight, we should like you to
have our reward after all," he said. "We
want you to get electricity, and be able to
play video games!"

"But –" hesitated Sir Garibald.

"Thank you!" cried Hot Nose, quickly accepting the money.

"You got rid of our dragon.

We want to give you a reward as well!" cried the Greenway villagers. And they did.

44

So Sir Garibald and Hot Nose had electricity put into the dark, creepy castle. It became a bright, uncreepy castle.

Sir Garibald had a great time, playing video games. He invited all the people (and especially the children) to come and play video games whenever they wanted to.

Hot Nose invited them, as well. He had a plan. Every time he won a game – which would be often, because he would practise a lot – the loser would give him a prize...